CARL DIPIETRO

12/05

Dear Big, Mean, Ugly Monster

by Ruth Marie Berglin

Illustrated by Carl DiRocco

Child & Family Press · Washington, DC

Child & Family Press is an imprint of the Child Welfare League of America. The Child Welfare League of America is the nation's oldest and largest membership-based child welfare organization. We are committed to engaging people everywhere in promoting the well-being of children, youth, and their families, and protecting every child from harm.

CHILD WELFARE LEAGUE OF AMERICA, INC.
HEADQUARTERS
440 First Street, NW, Third Floor, Washington, DC 20001-2085
E-mail: books@cwla.org

CURRENT PRINTING (last digit)
10 9 8 7 6 5 4 3 2 1

Text design by Jennifer R. Geanakos
Edited by Tegan A. Culler

Printed in the United States of America

ISBN 13: 978-1-58760-072-2
ISBN 10: 1-58760-072-2

Library of Congress Cataloging-in-Publication Data
Berglin, Ruth M.
  Dear big, mean, ugly monster / by Ruth M. Berglin ; illustrated by Carl DiRocco.
     p. cm.
  Summary: Joe is afraid of the monster that lives under his bed until they exchange letters and learn surprising things about each other.
  [1. Fear of the dark--Fiction. 2. Monsters--Fiction. 3. Bedtime--Fiction.] I. DiRocco, Carl, 1963- ill. II. Title.
PZ7.B452215De 2005
[E]--dc22
                                                    2005019502

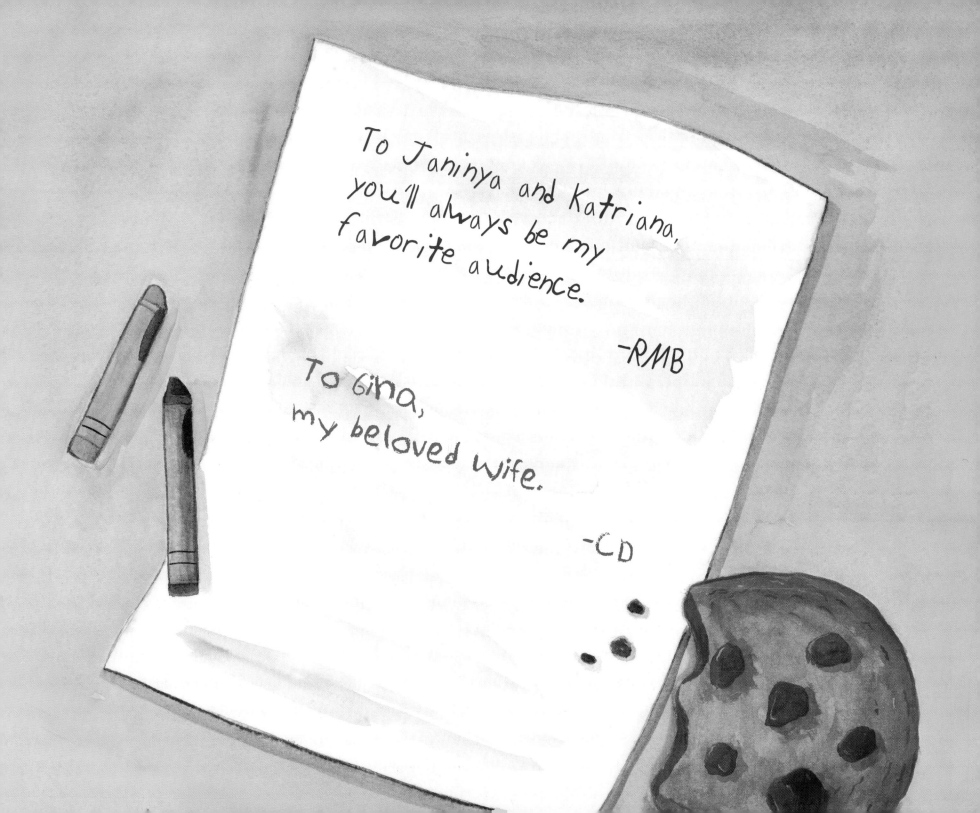

Joe was not afraid of very many things…

...but he *was*
afraid of monsters.

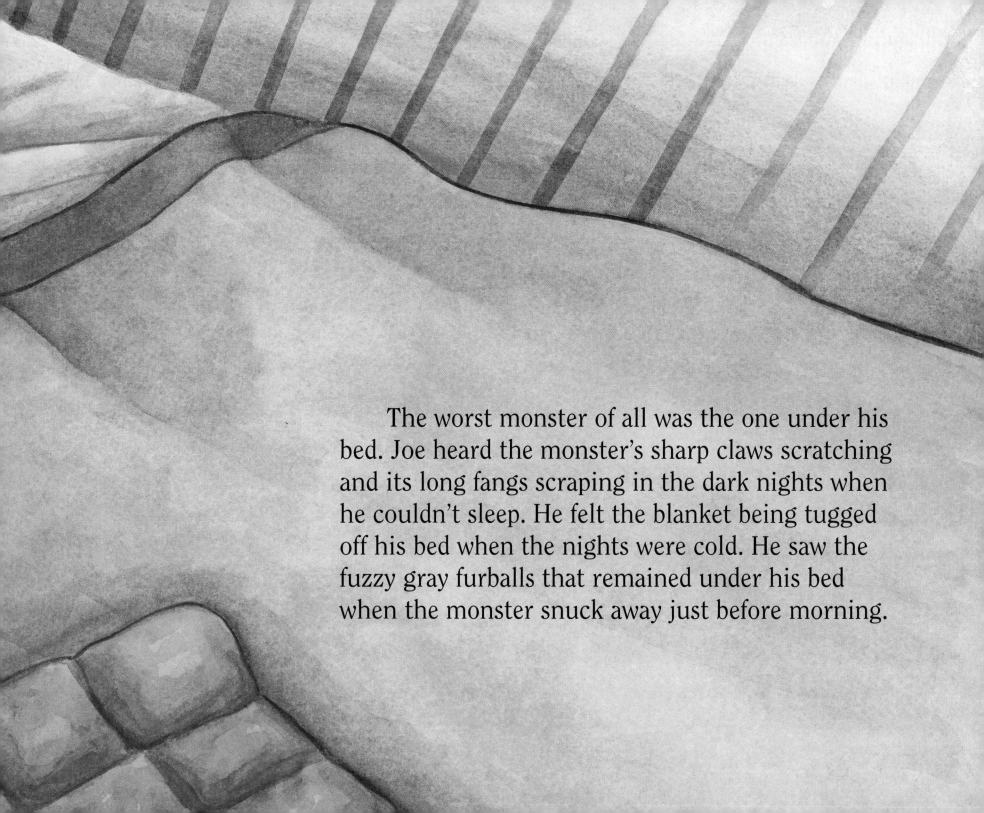

The worst monster of all was the one under his bed. Joe heard the monster's sharp claws scratching and its long fangs scraping in the dark nights when he couldn't sleep. He felt the blanket being tugged off his bed when the nights were cold. He saw the fuzzy gray furballs that remained under his bed when the monster snuck away just before morning.

Joe didn't like to get into bed after dark. Every night, he climbed on his chair, tiptoed across the top of his desk, jumped to the top of his dresser, and leaped to the safety of his bed. He knew this was the only way to keep the bloodthirsty monster from dragging him under the bed and having him for a snack.

Joe's mom tried to help. She gave him a squirt bottle full of green liquid. The words "MONSTER SPRAY" were boldly written on the side. But Joe still wondered. His mother had told him many times that she didn't see any monsters in his room. If she had not seen the monster, how did she know what kind of spray would chase it away? Maybe this monster was only afraid of purple spray. Or maybe pink?

Joe's dad gave him a flashlight for his birthday. He hoped it would make Joe less afraid. The problem was that it couldn't light the whole room. Joe worried that the monster would sneak up on him.

What if it came out of the dark corner by his chair while he was busy checking the closet?

The Three
Billy Goats
Gruff

Then one day, Joe's mom read a story about three goats who wanted to cross a bridge that was guarded by a horrible troll. The goats did not use sprays or flashlights to defeat the troll. They used their brains. They used words. What a great idea!

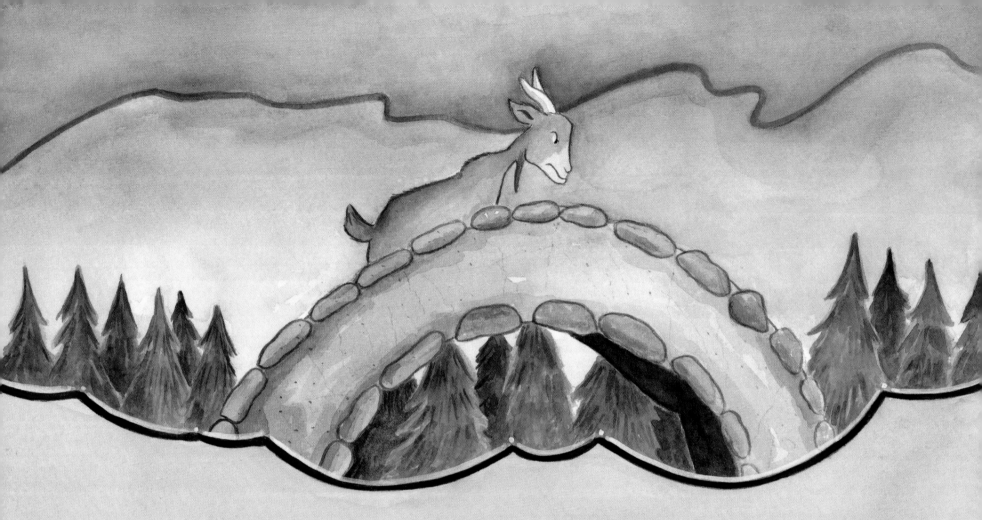

But unlike the two smaller goats,
Joe did not have any bigger brothers to
offer to the troll. And a face-to-face battle
like the biggest goat had with the troll
seemed pretty risky.

Joe decided to write a letter instead.
He took out his sharpest red crayon, and
the words spilled out.

He used lots of exclamation points because his teacher said that they meant the words were shouted. Maybe the shouting would scare the monster away. Joe carefully propped the note against one of the legs of the bed. He was sure the monster would see it that night while he waited for Joe.

Dear Big, Mean, Ugly Monster with Nasty Fangs and Long Fingernails,

I know you are waiting under my bed to get me. I am tired of walking across my desk and dresser to get to my bed! I'm tired of being cold because you pulled the blankets away. GO AWAY!! And don't ever come back!!!

Sincerely,
Joe

The monster *did* find the note. And he
was afraid. The words screamed at him from
the paper. Strong words. Angry words. Mean
words.

Quietly, shaking with fear, the monster
crept out from under the bed.

He looked over his shoulder
to be sure that Joe was still asleep.
Then, the monster quickly grabbed
a piece of paper and the green
crayon from Joe's desk. Hesitantly,
he began to write.

When Joe got up the next morning, he couldn't believe his eyes. Leaning against the box of crayons on his desk was a note.

Dear Joe,

Please don't hurt me. I'm sorry I make you so tired. I just go under your bed to hide. It is dark there. And safe. I use the blanket as my shield.

Sincerely,
SAM
(Sorta Average Monster)

P.S. I'm really not very big or mean, and I just need braces to fix my teeth.

Joe read the note three more times. Could this be real? Was the monster trying to trick him? The back of his neck itched, like someone was tickling him with a feather. Joe thought he could feel someone watching him. He rubbed the back of his neck, picked up his purple crayon, and wrote.

Joe put the note under his bed before the sun went down. He didn't want to meet SAM after dark. Even if he was a Sorta Average Monster.

When SAM found the note, he was
sad. Such mean words! And then SAM got
mad. Such unfair words! SAM grabbed the
red crayon and began to scribble some
angry words of his own.

Dear Joe,

Why do you call ME mean? You are the one who hunts and kills monsters. I have seen the bottle of Monster Spray on your dresser. I know that it is made from the blood of dead monsters. I've seen the light stick you use to surprise the monsters you hunt. I've heard you begging your mom to bake monster cookies for your snack. YOU are the one who is mean! I wish YOU would go away!!

Sincerely,

SAM

Joe found the note when he woke up the next morning. He was surprised. SAM thought Joe was mean? He couldn't believe it! But he did believe SAM was telling the truth. Thoughtfully, Joe picked up his green crayon and wrote.

Dear SAM,

I'm sorry I scared you. I know how icky it feels to be afraid. The Monster Spray is stuff my mom made for me. I think it is just water with food coloring. I have not tried it. The flashlight is not for hunting. I use it to read books in bed after bedtime. And monster cookies are just big cookies with lots of stuff in them. My mom makes them with extra chocolate chips. They are my favorite snack.

Sincerely,
Joe

When he read Joe's note, SAM was so relieved that he did a Happy Monster Dance:

He jumped into the air as high as he could, twirled around three times, and clicked his heels together, once to the left, and once to the right.

With a big grin on his face, he picked up his purple crayon and wrote:

Dear Joe,

Thanks for your note. It made me feel better. I like to read books, too. Reading is the most fun when I'm supposed to be sleeping. Have you read "The Three Billy Goats Gruff"? That is my favorite story. I have never tried monster cookies. My favorite food is bananas.

Sincerely,
SAM

Joe was not surprised to find the note by his crayon box this time. He was hoping SAM would write. SAM's note gave Joe an idea. Quickly, he picked up his blue crayon and wrote.

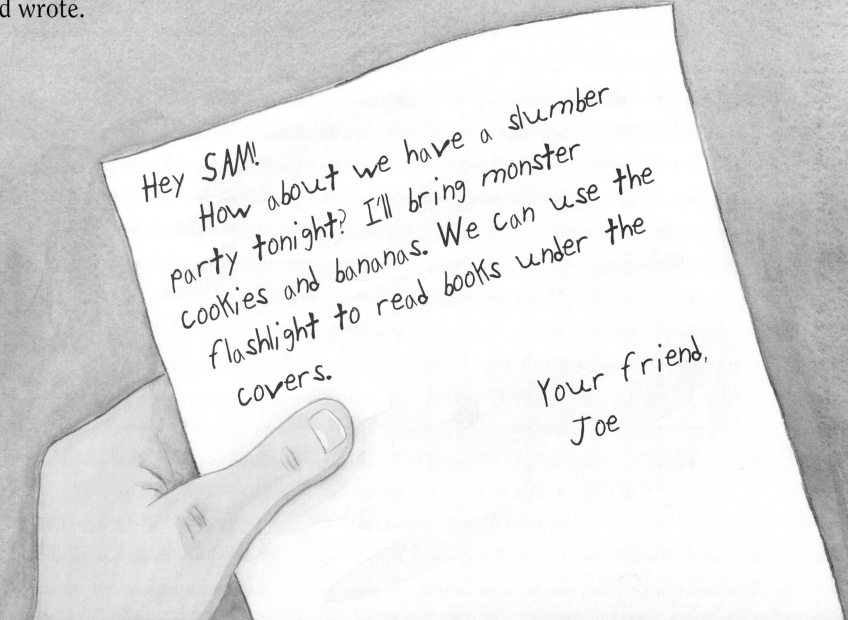

Hey SAM!
How about we have a slumber party tonight? I'll bring monster cookies and bananas. We can use the flashlight to read books under the covers.

Your friend,
Joe

And that is just what they did.